I Can Be a Doctor Too!

I Can Be a Doctor Too!

Dr Azjaah Rogers, MD

BYOB Movement Worldwide Consulting

Acknowledgements:

I would like to acknowledge the extraordinary individuals who have impacted every walk of my life both directly and indirectly, I am forever indebted to you all.

First and foremost, to my parents & step parents. You have all played a role in creating the foundation of life as I know it. To the two that brought me into the world, you literally gave me life, instilled nothing but greatness and made everything possible today. Thank you. And to the bonus parents that God felt should be placed in my life, thank you for taking on that role.

To my wonderful siblings, thank you all for being some of life's first best friends and teachers. You all have always supported me in every endeavor, thank you.

To my love, you have made experiencing life with you a joy. You are always pushing me to accomplish new tasks and strive toward greatness, thank you.

To my amazing friends, I couldn't imagine going through this process without you all! Thank you!

To my editor and author thank you for ensuring that everything was put together nicely and making my vision a reality, even if I had multiple requests!

To my mentors Dr. Shawna Hamilton and Dr. Tra'Chella Johnson-Foy, thank you for being both the inspiration and the blueprint. I couldn't have created this story without either of you.

Last but not least, thank you to the readers for choosing this book to be apart of your library. I hope it brings fulfillment!

Dr Azjaah Rogers, MD

I slightly open my eyes after hearing mama say "get up April, it's time for you to get ready for your doctor's appointment". I sit at the edge of my bed rubbing my eyes once more so that I can see clearly!

"Oh no, it's that time of year again already!?"

"Time to go to the doctor?"

I think to myself. Hey, I've been to the doctor seven years in a row, I know what to wear the eighth time around.

I go over to my drawer and pull out the thickest sweater I can find...my favorite winter sweater. The pink fluffy one with a retty sparkly unicorn in the middle. Then I grab the blue jeans match, it has two pretty unicorns on both front pockets covere in glitter.

I walk over to the mirror and begin smiling brightly once I notic my smooth, chestnut colored skin and this nice outfit I put together.

Now I have to ask mama to help me put my hair in those cute ponytails so I can add the unicorn headband to match!

"Mom, I'm ready for you to do my hair now."

Mama chuckled a little and said, "Aww baby, don't be scared; it'll be ok I promise. Now, go change into something lighter so you don't get too hot."

I change from my sweater into my blue short-sleeved unicorn shirt so at least I still match. And mama fixes m̃ hair into two puffy ponytails so we can go to the doctor

We walk outside and the hot air touches my cheeks as soon as I get one foot out the door. "I'm happy I changed my sweater." I think to myself! I can feel the breeze brush past my face, I can see the clear blue-sky dancing around the sun, the smell of fresh cut grass fills my nose and I hear birds singing for joy. Hmm maybe today won't be so bad I think to myself. At least, I hope not.

On the way to the doctor, I realize we take different streets than usual. As mama moves in and out of traffic there are cars everywhere! This time we also have to wai at a train track, The loud "chuga chuga choo choo" sound fills my ears before I even see the train!

Next, we see something that says "Metro Train Station" with lots of people waiting around. Finally, she drives pas some of the tallest buildings I've ever seen! I don't usuall see tall buildings going to the doctor so I say, "Hey mom, this isn't the way to the doctor!"

"Oh, April honey, I forgot to tell you that you're going to see a new doctor today.

Her name is Dr. Hamilton."

"Oh no, I hope she's nice mama."

We arrive at the doctor's office and mama has to open my car door for me because I really really didn't want to get out.

As soon as we walk into the office, I feel nervous again. My hands become a little sweaty. It's a different building but the smell of fear and the sound of kids crying were all too familiar.

We wait and we wait a little longer, which I didn't mind one bit!

While we wait, I look at everything around me and notice a green wall with pictures of giraffes, elephants, lions, tigers and much more painted all over the walls.

There was almost every animal you could think of in sight! It looked as if they were coming out of the wall to say hi to me! I love animals and I keep asking mama about getting a puppy, so this made me feel at home.

Finally, a young man with curly black hair calls out my name, "April Roberts." Mama gets up and I follow her lead

He introduces himself as Nurse Brian and tells mama and I that he helps Dr. Hamilton with the kids before she goes in to see them.

He does a lot of cool things that didn't hurt one bit, like making me stand on a "scale" that showed numbers. He asked me to sit and cover my eyes while I name shapes, and he let me lift my fingers when I heard music sounds which was so fun! I must admit, I like it here a little.

EYE CHART

The fun ended and he told us to wait for a second. This is usually when the shots come, so I cling on to mama for protection with my head on her shoulder.

She tries her best to make me feel better, and begins pointing at paintings of dogs on the wall in the room we were in.

"Oooo April, look at the pictures of all the different dogs in this room. This is probably the doggy room by the looks of it. You know you've been asking about getting a puppy a lot!"

There was a knock on the door, and I forgot about the dogs right away and put my head back onto mama's shoulder.

A tall, slender lady enters with the biggest smile I've ever seen. She was swaying from side to side dancing to her own tune! She's wearing a black dress with a long white coat on top of it!

She starts singing with her dance, "Good morning, good morning, good morning to you! It's soooo nice to meet you, we have so much to do."

Mama and I start laughing! Gee, I was not expecting that!

She told us her name was Dr. Hamilton and then begin to ask me questions about my favorite color, my favorite fruits and vegetables, my school, my favorite movies, and much more!

She made me feel special because we talked about all of the things I love to talk about!

I ask her "Dr. Hamilton, do I have to get shots today? I'm scared and I don't want any"

"Yes April, you have to get two shots before going to school in a few weeks, but since you're scared, I'll give you the shots myself so that I can make sure it's as gentle as possible.

If I hurt you, then you don't have to come see me anymore, deal?"
I agreed.

I smile back and say "Well that wasn't so bad after all! Maybe I won't be scared to come next year!"

We gather our stuff to leave, and Dr. Hamilton gave me a crown sticker along with a red lollipop! I was the happiest kid leaving the doctor's office!

We get in the car and drive away. I sat quietly for a little while and said to mama "I'm happy I went to that new doctor today, she was so nice and I can't believe she looked just like me!" "When I grow up, I want to be a superhero doctor just like her."

My mama said "April, always remember you can be whatever you want to be and I'm very happy you like your new doctor".

I sit back in my seat and smile because I learned two things about going to the doctor's office today: I am brave, and I can be a doctor too!

Lightning Source UK Ltd.
Milton Keynes UK
UKHW052201160522
403106UK00002B/7